W9-CAU-257

This book belongs to

_____

For added fun, find Sophie's friends on each

page, and fun facts for Mom and Dad too!

Have a book idea?

Contact us at:

Mascot Books
560 Herndon Parkway
Suite 120
Herndon, VA 20170

info@mascotbooks.com | www.mascotbooks.com

The True Story of Sophie la girafe ®

Copyright © 2012 by Jane Wood and Sophie la Girafe S.A.S

Sophie la girafe is the exclusive property of Sophie la Girafe S.A.S
and used with permission here.

© SOPHIE LA GIRAFE Modèle déposé / Design patent Sophie la girafe© :
Product protected by copyright (by order of the Paris court of appeal dated 30 June 2000).®

All rights reserved. No part of this publication may be reproduced or
transmitted in any form or by any means, electronic or mechanical,
including photocopy, recording, or any information storage and
retrieval system, without permission in writing from the publisher.

Requests for permission to make copies of any part of the work should
be submitted online at info@mascotbooks.com or mailed to Mascot
Books, 560 Herndon Parkway #120, Herndon, VA 20170.

PRW0515B

Printed in the United States

ISBN-13: 9781620860281
ISBN-10: 1620860287

www.mascotbooks.com

The True Story of

Sophie la girafe®

Jane Wood

Paris 1961

Sophie's Fun Facts:

The "Swinging Sixties" was a time of social revolution and, of course, a time of Beatle-mania!

O nce upon a time in Paris, a wonderful little giraffe was born. The year was 1961, and she was named Sophie. Shortly after she was born, Sophie moved to a small village in the French Alps. Sophie was very lucky to be born in the 1960s. A lot of exciting things were going on!

Sophie loved her home in the French Alps, but she wanted to see the world. It was time to travel! Her friend, Kiwi the bird, had told her about another country in Europe called Switzerland. Sophie decided that this would be her first stop. She could hardly sleep the night before she left. She was so excited!

Switzerland was the first foreign country Sophie had ever visited! The first thing she wanted to see was a cuckoo clock. A funny little bird came out of the clock chirping, "Cuckoo! Cuckoo! Cuckoo!" The bird reminded her of Kiwi. It made Sophie laugh!

Sophie's Fun Facts:

70% of Switzerland is covered in mountains. The average Swiss person eats 23 pounds of chocolate per year.

Sophie enjoyed the 1980s and 1990s in France and Switzerland. She loved spending time with all her friends.

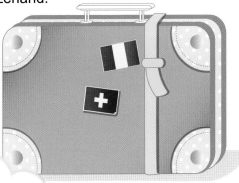

Europe was fun and very beautiful, but Sophie had itchy feet. She needed a new adventure. Sophie decided to visit her friend, Josephine the mouse, who was staying in New York City!

Sophie had to choose whether to take a boat or an airplane across the Atlantic Ocean. Kiwi loved flying and said, "Take a plane, Sophie! There's nothing like soaring in the sky."

Sophie wasn't so sure. "I've never flown before. Flying is normal for a bird like you, Kiwi, but it is not normal for a giraffe like me."

After a lot of thinking, Sophie decided to be brave, and booked a flight to New York City!

Sophie's Fun Facts:

The United States Hockey Team won the silver medal in the Olympics in 2002. Sophie prefers basketball, the perfect sport for a tall giraffe.

Sophie had a very nice flight and landed safely at John F. Kennedy Airport in New York City. Josephine was right there to meet her.

"It's time to show you the United States of America!" Josephine said happily.

Sophie had other ideas. "The long flight across the Atlantic Ocean and into a different time zone made me very sleepy," she said.

After a much needed nap, Sophie and Josephine set out to see the wonderful sights. From New York City to California, the friendly giraffe and lively mouse had a blast! Sophie really liked the Empire State Building and the huge Hollywood sign. Those large sights made the tall giraffe feel right at home.

Josephine wanted to show Sophie one more sight before she left the US: Mount Rushmore! The huge carving of former US presidents was amazing! During the tour, they learned all about how the artists were able to carve the mountain.

Sophie's Fun Facts:

There are over 150 castles in Germany, and over 300 kinds of bread.

BERLIN

Sophie met some very nice German tourists at Mount Rushmore. She became very interested in their home country and decided Germany would be her next stop.

Sophie saw a lot of interesting things in Germany. She saw Mercedes Benz and BMW cars, she tried many kinds of sausage, and she toured the beautiful city of Munich. Sophie even got to see the City of Berlin, the capital of Germany.

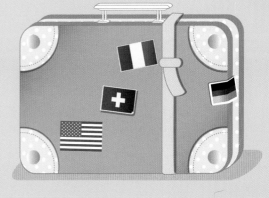

Sophie's Fun Facts:

About 6 million Canadians speak French.

After visiting Germany, Sophie flew back towards the US. She was heading to Canada, the United States' northern neighbour. Sophie visited the CN Tower in Toronto, Ontario. She was shocked to learn that the tower is 1,815 feet tall! For the first time in a long time, Sophie felt very short.

Sophie had seen lots of snow in Canada, so she decided to heat things up with a trip to the Italian coast !

Sophie loved Italy and even toyed with the idea of changing her name to Sophia. The countryside was beautiful and the food was delicious. Sophie tried spaghetti for the first time and it became her favourite food! An English tourist told her to try fish and chips if she was ever in England. "United Kingdom, here I come!" said Sophie.

Sophie's Fun Facts:

Ice cream is an Italian invention. In Italy they call it gelato.

Ristorante
— Italiano —

Sophie's Fun Facts:

The world's first public zoo was opened in 1829 in London.

Sophie's trip from Italy to the United Kingdom was a breeze! Travelling around Europe is very easy, even for a giraffe. Sophie's favorite things in London were the famous double-decker buses. Riding on the top was so much fun! The open roof let her stretch her long neck. It was so comfortable she didn't even mind the rain. Sophie was on holiday!

Sophie's Fun Facts:

The Great Barrier Reef is the longest reef in the world and covers 344,400 square kilometers or 133,000 square miles.

From Europe, Sophie flew to Australia on the other side of the world.

She loved seeing Ayr's Rock and meeting the Bushmen in the Outback. She also swam near the Great Barrier Reef. Sophie even learned how to surf!

Next, Sophie hopped on a plane and travelled from Australia to the Far East.
She especially wanted to see China and Japan.

In China, Sophie was amazed at the size of the Great Wall! It was one of the most
impressive sights she had seen so far.

Sophie's Fun Facts:

Every year, many athletes run The Great Wall
Marathon that spans 26.2 miles or 42.2 kilometers
along the wall. The Great Wall of China is 25
feet high in some places, and ranges from
15-30 feet wide.

After a very long walk along the Great Wall of China, it was time for Sophie to catch her short flight to Japan. The famous Japanese cherry blossoms took her breath away. Sophie felt like her bright colour paled in comparison to the beautiful flowers.

Sophie's Fun Facts:

Japan consists of over 6,800 islands.

After leaving the busy streets of Tokyo, the largest city in Japan, Sophie was ready for more exploring. She decided to head to Northern Europe and visit Norway, Sweden, and Denmark. These three countries, together with Iceland and Finland, are known as Scandinavia.

Sophie's Fun Facts:

25% of Finland lies within the Arctic Circle.
There are 1.8 million saunas in Finland.

The first thing Sophie did was take a tour of a Viking ship in Norway. Then, she ate meatballs in a Volvo in Sweden. Sophie's most memorable moment in Scandinavia was the hour she spent in a sauna in Finland. It was the perfect way for a tired, travelling giraffe to relax.

Although Sophie was having the time of her life, she started to feel a little homesick. She was tired of living out of a suitcase. It was a lovely case with stickers from all the places she had been, but Sophie missed her friends Chan, Pie, and Gnon. It was time for this little giraffe to head back to France.

Sophie has a special place in her heart for Paris. She was glad to be back in France. She decided it was time to take another peek at the Mona Lisa in the Musée du Louvre.

Sophie loved being back in her home country.
"Home, sweet home," she sighed.

Sophie had seen so many amazing things and met so many nice people on her trip around the world. She knew she was very lucky to have been on such an incredible journey. It turned out to be a journey of a lifetime!

But there was still more of this wonderful world to see. Sophie couldn't wait! There are so many countries, and each one has its own, magical sights.

Until next time,
stay safe and
be ready for the
next adventures
of Sophie la girafe...